Book Three

Kudzu Monsters Versus The Creeper Horde

J.R. HARDIN

Published in the USA by:
Boutique of Quality Books Publishing Company
www.boutiqueofqualitybooks.com

Printed in the United States of America
ISBN 978-0-9828689-8-0

Library of Congress Control Number: 2010918360

Book & cover design by Darlene Swanson • www.van-garde.com
Cover illustration by Steve McGinnis • www.digraphics.info

Other Books by J.R. Hardin

THE KUDZU MONSTERS
Published in June 2010

KALVIN THE KUDZU MONSTER
Published in October 2010

LITTLE DOG KOKO
Coming in summer of 2011

Contents

Introduction

In my first two books I told the readers about kudzu and how it came to America. I mentioned how it spread over millions of acres of land in the southeastern states. In this book I'd like to mention a few of its good properties.

Kudzu leaves are nutritious and are feed to farm animals. A farmer in North Carolina makes bales of kudzu hay to feed his cattle. Another farmer has a herd of goats that feed on the kudzu leaves and kudzu blossom jelly and syrups are made in the south. Kudzu cookbooks include deep-fried kudzu leaves, kudzu quiche, kudzu candies, jelled desserts and many other recipes.

Medicines for pet hamsters and mice are made from kudzu. Harvard Medical School research led to a drug made from kudzu roots that may help in the treatment of alcoholism. Ground kudzu roots have been used in foods and medicines for several centuries in Japan and China.

Basket makers like the long flexible kudzu vines for weaving baskets and other forms of vine art. Some people make paper products from kudzu.

Many people make a living from the products made from kudzu vines.

Acknowledgments

I wish to thank my sister, Betty Hertenstein, for editing my books and for the contributions she's made to my stories.

I would like to thank my publisher, Terri Ann Leidich, for all she has done to promote my books.

Also I wish to thank Darlene Swanson my book designer for the excellent job she has done.

Lastly I would like to thank Steve McGinnis for creating my exciting book cover.

Chapter One

The Journey Begins

Kalvin stood in the forest with his sister Kandi and watched a young human named Maranda run toward them. Kandi and Maranda were good friends even though Kandi was a kudzu monster. Maranda was nearly fourteen and Kandi was almost three, but Kandi and Maranda were both five feet tall. A little squirrel named Sparkle sat on Kandi's shoulder and nervously flipped her tail.

"Hi, Maranda," said Kandi. "Did you have a nice Christmas?"

"Oh, yes, I received a lot of presents. Mom gave me two new dresses and a sweater and Dad gave me a computer. And I had presents under the Christmas tree from other people, too."

"What's a computer?" asked Kalvin.

"It's an electronic machine that does all kinds of

things," answered Maranda. "I can look up things on the Internet or play games."

"What's the Internet?" asked Kandi.

"I'll explain all that later. I see Dad coming. He has some presents for you and your family."

"These humans scare me," whispered Sparkle.

"It's all right; they're friends," answered Kandi.

"What's that murmuring sound?" Maranda asked. "Did you make that noise?"

"Yes," Kandi replied. "We communicate with small forest animals in that low tone. The animals understand the words in their own language. We also understand their speech when they chatter or squeak at us."

"Do you make different sounds for each type of animal?" asked Maranda.

"No," answered Kalvin. "When we talk to a group of different animals they hear us in their own language."

"We don't know how we do it," added Kandi. "It's just the way we were created."

"Can a squirrel talk to a rabbit?" asked Maranda.

"Yes," answered Kalvin. "I don't understand how they do it either. They touch noses and get their message across. Maybe they can read each other's thoughts by touching noses."

Maranda's father carried a large box and made a grunting noise as he placed it on the ground in front of Kalvin.

"Hello, Kalvin and Kandi. That is one heavy box. Maranda tells me that your family and other kudzu monsters will fight those creeper creatures again this spring. I bought you some things you can use to defend yourselves."

He opened the box and took out four axes, a hatchet and a couple of things that looked like thick-bladed axes on one side and sledge hammers on the other side.

"I figured that Kalvin and Kitty could use the axes, Kleatus could use the heavier mauls, and the hatchet is for Kandi. The store only had two axes that had a blade on each side, so I got those and two regular axes."

Kandi picked up her hatchet and examined the sharp blade. Kalvin picked up a double-bladed axe and a regular axe, but he had trouble wrapping his tentacles around the handles.

"It looks like the handles are too thin for large kudzu monsters to hold," said Maranda's father. "I'll nail and glue some pieces of wood to the sides and make the handles thicker."

Kalvin and Kandi thanked him for the presents. Maranda's father carried the axes and mauls into the barn to work on them.

Kalvin stayed in the woods and watched Kandi until she was ready to leave. It was still daylight so they had to move carefully through the bare trees. They didn't want other humans to spot them.

"Kalvin," said Kandi, "I'm getting scared now that spring is approaching. I'm afraid of the creepers."

"I'm scared too, Kandi, but we have to stop their migration north."

"Why do the kudzu monsters have to fight them every time they come north? There are so few of us to face so many of those creatures."

"I know, Kandi, but humans are the only other ones strong enough to defeat them and the creepers avoid them. The creatures would sneak past them and continue to kill our animal friends. Besides, a group of creepers might catch one of us by surprise and kill us. We stand a better chance by attacking them as a group before they can attack us individually."

"I think we need more kudzu monsters than we had last year."

"I agree with you," answered Kalvin. "The more monsters we have, the better our chance of survival."

When Kalvin and Kandi returned home, they told their parents all about their visit with the humans and the weapons Maranda's father was preparing for them. Kandi found a limb that had split from a tree and made a four-foot spear from it with her hatchet.

By the end of January the monsters had their modified weapons plus an additional three axes for other kudzu monsters. Kleatus swung his heavy mauls as easily as a grown man could swing a fly swatter. Kalvin and Kitty had one regular axe and one double-bladed axe apiece. They were ready for the battle but had to wait until early March before starting their journey to Karrie's hill, where they faced the creepers the year before.

They had talked last year about joining their friends Karl and Karen before heading toward Karrie, but it was decided that six kudzu monsters traveling together would draw too much attention.

Kalvin and his family left in early March and traveled through the forest mostly at night. Their squirrel friends, Squiggy and Sparkle, had insisted on coming with them. Squiggy always rode on Kalvin's upper left arm and Sparkle rode on Kandi's. The squirrels climbed trees and watched for humans when the monsters slept. When they traveled during the day, the squirrels scouted the territory in front of them. Kalvin and his family had an uneventful journey and arrived at Karrie's in mid-March.

Kleatus and Kitty chopped down some small trees to make stout clubs for Karrie and the other monsters.

"Kalvin, I have a mission for you," said Karrie. "I need you to find a very old and very large kudzu monster named Koda. My fox, Charlie, will go with you. He knows the area where Koda usually dwells. You must tell him that the creeper queen will be here soon with her army."

"I'll find him," replied Kalvin, "and bring him here before the creepers arrive."

"Don't be frightened of him; he may sound gruff, but he'll help us. Koda is my father."

Chapter Two

The Search for Koda

"Charlie, have you ever met Koda?" asked Kalvin.

"I went with Karrie one time when she visited him," answered Charlie.

"What is he like? Karrie said I shouldn't be afraid of him."

"He's very large. Karrie said he's close to thirty-five feet tall and he has ten arm tentacles. You'll really need his help when you fight the creeper horde."

"How does he move through the forest? Being that large he'd have a hard time going between the trees."

"Koda doesn't move much. He stayed rooted to the ground the week I visited him with Karrie. He sleeps most of the time. Karrie had to hit him with a rock to wake him."

Kalvin only carried the twin-bladed axe in his lower right arm tentacle and gave the other axe to Karrie until he returned. Squiggy rode on Kalvin's upper left shoulder most of the time. Occasionally he would climb up a tree to talk with other squirrels.

"We've been traveling east for four days," Charlie told Kalvin. "We're getting close to where Koda lives. You wait on top of this hill. I can search this area much faster on my own."

Charlie trotted into the forest and disappeared from sight very quickly.

"Squiggy, look around for other squirrels," Kalvin requested. "Ask them if they know where Koda dwells."

Squiggy scampered into the woods and quickly climbed a tall oak tree. Kalvin sent feeder roots into the ground and began to draw nourishment from the soil. About an hour later Squiggy returned and climbed up to Kalvin's ear slot.

"None of the squirrels have seen Koda in over a year," Squiggy reported. "I'll climb that tall poplar tree and look for Charlie."

Two hours later Kalvin heard Squiggy barking excitedly from the top of the tree.

"What's wrong, Squiggy?" Kalvin shouted. "What do you see? I can't understand your chattering."

Squiggy ran down the tree until he was close to Kalvin.

"I spotted Charlie. He's about a quarter of a mile away and he's running from something."

"Climb a little higher and see if you can tell what's chasing him."

Squiggy climbed about fifteen feet higher. "It looks like a pack of dogs to me."

Charlie crested the hill. Panting heavily, he barely got out that coyotes were chasing him. Just then a coyote charged up the hill and chomped down on Charlie's left rear paw. As Charlie howled from the pain, Kalvin's lower left arm tentacle wrapped around the coyote. Releasing Charlie, the coyote yipped as Kalvin lifted him several feet above the ground. He hurled the coyote into two of his buddies that had topped the hill. All three of them bounced down the hill. Two others stopped when three of their brother coyotes tumbled past them. Howling and yipping, the five coyotes fled into the forest.

"Thanks, Kalvin," Charlie whispered. "I'm out of breath running from the coyotes. I thought they'd eat me for sure."

"You're welcome. How's your foot?"

"A little sore, but I'll be okay," Charlie insisted.

"Did you find Koda?"

"He wasn't down there," answered Charlie. A raccoon told me I might find him in the next valley."

They rested there the rest of the day and continued their journey around midnight. Charlie was limping, so he stayed close to Kalvin for protection. In the morning they reached the valley. Squiggy learned Koda's location from the other squirrels and a few hours later they stood before Koda's massive form.

"He's asleep," chattered Squiggy. "I'll climb up to his ear slot and bark loudly."

"I don't think that's a good idea," Charlie warned.

Squiggy ran up Koda anyway and started barking in his ear. Koda didn't open his eyes, but an upper arm tentacle slapped Squiggy off his shoulder. Squiggy went flying through the air and grabbed a tree branch before he fell to the ground.

"Wake up!" Kalvin shouted. But Koda continued to sleep. Kalvin looked around and spotted a dead tree limb on the ground. He picked it up and swung it at one of Koda's foot tentacles.

"Aaaah!" roared Koda as his eyes popped open. "Who woke me up from my rest?" He looked down and spotted Kalvin. "Young monster why did you disturb me?" Koda rumbled.

"I'm sorry I had to wake you, but Karrie needs your

help," shouted Kalvin. "The creeper queen is coming with her army."

"Ah, the queen is back. Maybe this time we can kill her and stop her migration north. It might take me awhile to pull free of my feeder roots. I haven't moved in two years, and the roots are deep in the earth."

Koda pushed up with his mighty feet tentacles, and Kalvin could see that some of the feeder roots were three inches thick. Koda rocked from side to side and most of the roots broke free.

"Does it hurt to break the feeder roots when they're so thick?" Kalvin asked.

"The thick ones sting a little when they break loose," Koda shrugged.

Fifteen minutes later Koda began to move his three-ton body. Although most of Koda's feet tentacles were around fifteen feet long, he only moved about one mile an hour. He tried not to crush too many plants as he weaved his way through the forest.

"I was told you had ten arms," shouted Kalvin. "But I only count eight."

"I have a couple of branches on my upper body that get mistaken for arms."

"Have you always been this large?" Kalvin asked.

"No, I kept growing for seventy-five years. Most monsters stop after sixty years, except for Karrie. She stopped growing after forty years. When I was sixty, I was a little taller than Karl. Then I had rapid growth for another fifteen years. I don't know why."

Kalvin studied Koda as he lumbered along. Koda had three arms located a little over twenty feet from the ground. The one on his back nearly touched the ground and was about a foot thick at its base. The two in the front were nearly as thick and close to twenty feet long. Five shorter tentacles were scattered over his upper body. No kudzu leaves were growing on the top eight feet of his body.

Koda told Kalvin stories when they rested. Most of the tales were about the forest when he was young.

"Eighty or ninety years ago," Koda told him, "the forest was much larger and many more animals lived in it. My first animal companion was a fox like Charlie. I tried a possum for a while, but they're not very good at communicating. Possums have a short memory and they're slow. Foxes and squirrels make the best companions, if you can find a good squirrel."

"Squiggy is a good squirrel," answered Kalvin. "And his daughter Sparkle is just as smart."

"My fox was named Bart," Koda replied. "The creeper queen killed him seventy years ago. I chased her into a large lake and when she came out a month later I chased her all the way to Florida. I lost her in the swamps."

Koda crumpled a log in one of his arm tentacles as he recalled that memory.

"We've talked long enough," boomed Koda. "We don't want to be late for the battle."

They resumed their journey. Despite Koda's desire to hurry, it still took them longer to return to Karrie's hill because of his enormous size. After seven days they arrived, and Charlie wasn't limping anymore. While they had been gone, another monster had arrived at Karrie's that Kalvin had never seen before.

Chapter Three

Kokamo

The new monster slowly moved toward Kalvin.

"Hi," he said. "My name is Kokamo. You must be Kalvin."

"Hello," responded Kalvin. "Karrie told us you helped her fight the creeper scouts two years ago. I'm glad you're here to help us fight the creeper queen and her horde."

Kokamo had arrived a day after Kalvin was gone. He was twice Kalvin's age and stood about eighteen feet tall. His body was as thick as Karl's body, which gave him a stocky appearance. Kokamo carried two rusty-looking, twin-bladed axe heads that were jammed onto tree limbs and tied on with kudzu vines.

"Where did you get the axes?" asked Kalvin.

"I found these axe heads in an old abandoned lumber camp that caught fire over twenty years ago," answered

Kokamo. "The handles were burned up in the fire, so I used some tree limbs for handles. The axe heads weren't on the limbs securely, so Kandi wound kudzu vines around them. Your sister's small arm tentacles are good at tying."

"Can I have everyone's attention?" Karrie announced. "We need to round up as many of our forest friends as we can and inform them of the creeper invasion. It'll be morning soon and the animals will be up. Bring squirrels, rabbits, raccoons, possums, foxes and any other small animals that will listen to us."

As soon as the sun was up, the monsters scattered and talked to all the animals they could find, instructing them to come to Karrie's hill. By noon hundreds of animals were on the hill to listen to Karrie.

"Thank you for coming," Karrie shouted to the gathering of monsters and animals. "What I'm going to tell you could save your life and the lives of your family. Some terrible creatures known as creepers will be invading our forest in a few weeks. These creatures will eat any animals they can catch, so be on the lookout for them. They usually travel at night, but don't count on it. If you come close to them during the day, they will try to kill you. The creepers move very slowly, like kudzu monsters do, so you can run away from them and they can't catch you."

"What do these creatures look like?" asked a raccoon.

"They are several feet long and covered with shaggy grayish moss," answered Karrie. She knew that the animals only saw things in black and white and wouldn't understand greenish-gray moss or yellow eyes.

"The creepers have long tentacles that look like thick leafy vines. Beware; they can climb trees, so you won't be safe in your nests. You'll have to keep alert at night. If you spot a creeper, tell the kudzu monster nearest to you. We'll be awake and watching at night."

"Where do these creatures come from?" asked a fox.

"Many years ago Koda chased some creepers through the swamps of South Georgia and lost them in the Florida swamps where I suspect their home is located. There might be more tribes of creepers in other southern states, but I've never heard of any. I don't know why they migrate north every thirty or forty years. The queen creeper gives birth to all her creepers. If we could kill the queen, the other creepers would die out."

Kalvin noticed that beavers and otters had come from the lakes and streams to hear Karrie.

"What if the creepers don't come this way?" asked Kalvin. "What if they travel a different route north?"

"The creepers are creatures of habit," answered Karrie. "They travel the same paths if they can. If a new human community is in their path, they will move around it at night. They don't want to alert the humans. They know the humans have flashlights and rifles and could kill them very quickly. The kudzu monsters have stopped the creepers and destroyed most of them before. We can stop them again."

When the meeting was over, the forest animals disappeared into the woods and underground burrows.

"I didn't tell the small animals that we couldn't stop them without injury," said Karrie. "I didn't want to panic them into stampeding the first time a creeper shows up in the forest. The creepers will travel through here somewhere in a five-mile wide area. Koda can take the middle of the area and the rest of us will be on either side of him. Kleatus will be a half mile away on his right and Karl will be a half mile away on his left. Kitty will be half a mile to the right of Kleatus. Karen will be half of a mile away from Karl's left and so on. Kalvin will be on the end of the right side and I'll be on the end of the left side. Every monster will have a squirrel, fox or small animal with him or her to run messages. Other forest animals will be scattered around each monster, so that the creepers can't sneak past us."

"Where will Kandi be located?" asked Kitty.

"Kandi will be at the top of some cliffs above the large

lake," answered Karrie. She will have the safest position with a good view of the surrounding countryside."

"Who will be closest to Kandi?" asked Kleatus.

"Kalvin will be about five hundred yards in front and to the left of Kandi," replied Karrie.

Kitty and Kleatus were satisfied that Kandi was in the best position of all the monsters. Karrie also told them about a ranger tower on the other end of the lake from Kandi. The creepers would stay away from the tower.

Squiggy would be Kalvin's message carrier and Sparkle was with Kandi. That night the monsters began their watch. Everything was quiet that night and for every night after for the next two weeks.

Chapter Four

Creeper Watch

Reports came in during the third week of April that creeper scouts had been spotted a few miles south of the monsters but none of the creepers came close to the kudzu monsters. The creepers would survey the area then return south again. Kalvin was getting nervous and he was sure the other monsters and forest animals were as tense as he was.

In the last week of May reports came in that several beavers had been killed, and two small creepers died in an underwater battle at a large pond. Other reports came in that dozens of creepers had moved to within a mile of the monsters.

Kalvin was patrolling his area one night when he heard squirrels barking in the trees a couple of hundred yards south of his location. He moved toward the noise.

"Squiggy, tell the squirrels around me to keep a sharp

watch. I don't want to walk into a creeper trap like I did last year."

Squiggy raced around the forest and barked out the message to the other squirrels. Kalvin continued to move forward cautiously. There was only a half moon in the sky, but he could see very well in the dark forest. Kalvin spotted the shaggy shape of a creeper about a yard long as it climbed a tree near a squirrel nest. The mother squirrel stood between the creeper and her babies. Her tail was fluffed up and her teeth were bared. Kalvin moved closer to the tree. He was only fifty feet away when the creeper grabbed the mother squirrel and pulled her toward its mouth. Kalvin stretched back his arm and hurled the single-bladed axe at the creeper. The axe struck the creeper before it had time to eat the mother squirrel pinning the creature to the tree. Two other creepers dropped from other tree limbs and fled into the forest. Kalvin followed them for a while before returning to the tree where he had killed the creeper.

Oh, boy, thought Kalvin. My axe and the creeper are twenty feet up the tree and I'm only twelve feet tall. Kalvin stretched his upper right arm as high as he could reach but was still four feet too low. *I need something to knock the axe loose. Kalvin found a tree branch but could only hit the tip of the axe handle. Drat! The axe is buried into the tree too deep. I guess I'll have to throw the branch at the axe until I can knock it loose.*

"Squiggy, go tell Mom about the creeper attack while I try to free my axe and be careful. There might be creepers between Mom and me."

Squiggy ran to a tree and leaped through the treetops toward Kalvin's mom. Kalvin continued to throw the branch. The axe was slowly beginning to pull free.

Suddenly, a weasel ran up to Kalvin and barked a warning. All the other animals were watching Kalvin and failed to see four large creepers sneaking up on him. Thankfully, the weasel's sharp eyes had spotted the creepers.

Kalvin backed away from the tree so he could swing his axe. His first swing chopped the closest creeper in half. The other three spread out and began to move toward Kalvin on three sides. The creeper to his right moved next to the tree where the dead creeper was pinned by Kalvin's axe. At that moment the axe came loose from the tree and fell on the creeper standing below. The axe blade stuck in its head. Then the dead creeper fell from the tree onto the axe, driving the blade deeper. Kalvin bent over and pulled the axe from the creeper's head.

He turned to face the last two creepers, but the sight of the axe and the dead creeper falling from the tree had freaked them out. The other two creepers fled into the dark forest.

By the end of the first week of May fifteen creepers

had been killed by the kudzu monsters but a number of squirrels, rabbits, possums and hundreds of nesting birds had lost their lives to the creepers.

One night Kalvin spotted a group of eight creepers on his left headed toward his mom's location.

"Squiggy," Kalvin said, "go tell Mom that eight creepers are headed her way. I can't leave my position unless she needs help."

Squiggy headed toward Kitty. Kalvin turned to look behind him at the cliffs near the large lake. *I can't leave Kandi unprotected*, he thought. *She's bigger and stronger than she was last year, but she can't fight a group of creepers by herself.*

Kalvin turned back toward the forest listening for sounds of a battle. Squiggy had returned after informing Kitty of the creepers, but hours passed and Kalvin never heard any battle noises. When the sun came up, Kalvin relaxed. A new group of animals replaced the animals that had stayed up all night with Kalvin.

"Squiggy, I'm going to sleep for a bit while the sun is up. Tell the forest animals to keep a sharp watch while I sleep."

All the kudzu monsters slept a few hours while the sun was shining. The chances of a creeper attack were less during the daylight hours. Kalvin slept till a couple of hours past noon when he awoke to the chattering of a squirrel.

"What's wrong?" asked Kalvin.

"There's a battle happening near Koda," squealed the squirrel.

Kalvin could see signs of a battle two miles away to his left. Birds were circling Koda's position, and there were faint sounds of creeper shrieks mixed with deep monster roars. The sounds of battle stopped a few minutes later.

An hour later Rascal the raccoon, Kitty's messenger, trotted toward Kalvin and looked up at him.

"Your mom wanted me to tell you that a group of creepers attacked Koda while he was sleeping," the raccoon reported. "The animals around Koda couldn't wake him until the creepers were on him."

"Was Koda hurt by the creepers?" Kalvin asked.

"I don't know. All we know is that he got jumped by them while he was snoozing."

"Thanks," said Kalvin. "Go back to my mom and tell her thanks for the report."

The raccoon swaggered into the forest at a slow pace. *I guess he must be worn out from running. I hope Koda is okay. I can't imagine the creepers doing much damage to him.*

Late that evening Kalvin saw Charlie the fox trotting toward him.

"Well," said Charlie when he was near Kalvin, "about twenty creepers jumped Koda while he was sleeping."

"What happened?" Kalvin asked. "Was Koda hurt?"

"Koda had a few bites on him, but nothing serious. He's just too big. When Kleatus and Karl arrived, eight of the creepers were dead. Koda was picking creepers off his body and slamming them into the ground. Kleatus told me he saw Koda slap a creeper off the ground with that huge back arm of his. The creeper sailed through the air a hundred feet before it wrapped around a tree forty feet above the ground."

"I guess they'll stay clear of Koda from now on," Kalvin replied.

"Yeah, only four of the creepers escaped."

Chapter Five

Creeper Scouts

That night a possum scurried toward Kalvin.

"A large group of critters are headed your way," he reported. "You should probably run for it before they arrive."

"Thanks," answered Kalvin. "You did a good job."

The possum lumbered off behind Kalvin.

By critters I guess he meant creepers. I wish I knew what a large group is to him. It could be four or forty.

"Squiggy, go tell Mom I'll probably need help. Then return and keep a sharp lookout for creepers on the way."

Forest animals fled past him. Kalvin tightened his grip on his axes and backed into deep shadows. *I don't know how well creepers can see in the dark. I hope these shadows can hide me until I spot them first.*

A thicket about two hundred feet wide was between the woods where Kalvin was hidden and the forest where the creepers were. A field mouse squealed as a creeper snatched it off the ground. Kalvin didn't see or hear the mouse again.

It's hard to tell the creeper legs from the shrubs in the thicket. I do see some yellow creeper eyes in the forest. I count four pair of eyes there and I think another three are in the thicket. That's seven creepers I can see and there may be more. I hope Squiggy is careful. I wish Mom was here.

Kalvin glanced back toward the cliff where Kandi should be, but he couldn't see her. *I guess Kandi is hidden. She probably knows creepers are close.* He waited and watched for another half an hour. He saw little movement in the field, but more dark shadows crept into the forest. Kalvin heard a squirrel squeal. *I hope that wasn't Squiggy.* Just then Squiggy ran up to his shoulder and whispered in his ear slot.

"Kitty can't come," Squiggy told him. "She and Kleatus are fighting a dozen creepers as we speak. Your mom says for you not to engage the creepers until they get here."

"Don't worry," replied Kalvin. "I don't know how many creepers are out there."

Kalvin spotted a fourth creeper in the thicket when it grabbed and ate a snake. Two more creepers got in a fight over a turtle they grabbed at the same time.

I don't think their teeth can bite through a turtle shell.

But that makes six in the thicket, and I can see a dozen pairs of yellow eyes in the forest. I feel so helpless. Reptiles and animals are being eaten and I can't do anything because there are too many creepers.

Squirrels chattered and barked fifty feet to his left. Kalvin searched the dark for movement. A creeper grabbed at a squirrel and missed him by inches. Another creeper snatched a bird from its nest. Kalvin inched backwards very slowly. He bumped into a tree and a rotting branch fell to the ground. The branch sounded like a tree falling to Kalvin, and four pairs of yellow eyes turned his way.

Kalvin backed away at a faster rate of speed as he kept his eyes on the advancing creepers. He glanced at the thicket and the forest behind it. He didn't see any more of them headed his way.

Just then he felt a tentacle grab his leg. Turning he saw a creeper and swung his double-bladed axe. The blade sliced into the creature and killed it. He pulled his axe free and looked around. Kalvin didn't see the yellow eyes of the other three creepers. He turned in a circle but couldn't spot them anywhere.

They're out there somewhere, he thought. Three of them wouldn't run off at the sight of one of them getting killed.

"Squiggy, do you see any creepers moving near us," Kalvin whispered.

"I can't see much of anything," squeaked Squiggy. "But I hear something noisy in the trees."

Kalvin looked up in the trees and spotted a creeper moving along a limb above his head. The creeper dropped from a tree branch on Kalvin's right shoulder. Luckily Squiggy was on Kalvin's left shoulder. Kalvin dropped the axe from his upper right arm, reached up and grabbed the creeper before it could bite his face. He threw the creature to the ground as his lower right arm picked up his axe and sunk the blade deep into the creepers' back.

The third creeper sprang up from the bushes near his feet as the fourth creeper jumped on his back. Kalvin swung at the creeper near his feet tentacles first and finally hit it with his single-bladed axe as the other creeper on his back dropped to the ground. Kalvin turned to face the creeper that had attacked him from behind. The creeper was dead with a hatchet sticking in its head. Kandi stepped out of the shadows and pushed toward Kalvin.

"Nice throw with the hatchet," said Kalvin. "Why didn't you throw your spear instead?"

"I forgot I had the spear," answered Kandi. "I saw the creeper open his mouth to bite you and I just threw what was in my right arm tentacle."

"Let's move further from that thicket before the other creepers spot us," Kalvin whispered.

Kalvin and his sister moved to the top of a small hill where they could see the thicket and forest. Kalvin heard something large moving up the hill behind them. Kandi must have heard it too, because she turned at the same time Kalvin did.

"Kandi, what are you doing down here?" whispered Kitty.

"Mom, you scared me to death!" Kalvin said in a little louder voice.

"Kalvin, hold your voice down," Kitty warned. "There are too many creepers down there."

"I saw creepers attacking Kalvin and came down to help," Kandi replied.

"Where is Dad?" asked Kalvin.

"Kleatus went to help Koda, Karl and Kokamo. They were engaged in a fight with fifty or more creepers."

"What happened to the creepers you and Dad were battling?" Kalvin asked.

"We killed a couple of them and then the rest of them took off. They probably joined the creepers that Koda and the others are fighting."

Kalvin, Kitty and Kandi continued to observe the creepers during the night. The creepers didn't move out of the thicket.

"They seem to be waiting in the thicket for some rea-son," said Kitty. "I'm going back to my post. Kalvin, you go with Kandi to the top of the cliffs. I don't think it's safe for you down here."

Chapter Six

The Campers

Kalvin and Kandi took turns resting the rest of the night and through the morning. By noon Kalvin felt well rested.

"Kandi, I've been up here all morning. You stay up here and rest some more. Sparkle can keep watch for you. I'm going down to get a closer look and try to figure out what they are planning."

"Kalvin, be careful. I think Mom was right; they're up to something. Don't let them lure you into a trap."

"Don't worry, Kandi, he replied. "I know how they like to set traps."

Great, now my three-year-old sister is giving me advice. It's not like I have "Big Dummy" carved on my head.

Kalvin grumbled to himself as he came down the hill

and entered the wooded area near the thicket where he saw a creeper sleeping. The creature's body looked flatter on the ground. Its legs went up and back down to form arcs. He could see a large number of creeper legs criss-crossing each other in the thicket. Kalvin couldn't see any of the creatures in the forest beyond the thicket but he spotted the body of one of the creepers he'd killed last night. The body had gone flat and looked like a patch of shaggy grass. Its legs looked like dried reeds. The body didn't look like a creeper at all.

The creepers are all probably sleeping. I wonder if creepers sleep with their legs bowed up to form a barrier.

A large patch of the thicket seemed to move. A ripple slowly moved through the field of tangled reeds and vine-covered shrubs. Kalvin couldn't tell if it was a large group of creepers moving or a wind blowing through. He continued to stare at the spot after the movement stopped.

Something slid through the brush on the edge of the thicket and headed in his direction. Kalvin tensed. He was ready for any sudden attack by the creepers. An otter popped his head up and looked around; he saw Kalvin and scurried toward him.

"Several families of humans are camped a little distance from you," reported the otter. "They put up tents. The men and women are fishing while several children are swimming in the lake."

"Thanks for the information," Kalvin replied. "Stay clear of the thicket. Dozens of creepers are hidden in there."

The creepers in the forest are probably hiding from the humans, Kalvin thought. *The ones in the thicket won't move very far if humans are close. I think it will be okay for me to leave and check out the humans.*

Kalvin looked at the cliff top and was relieved to see Kandi standing there above the lake. *I'm glad she didn't come down to spy on the human kids. It must be killing her to stay on top of the cliffs.*

Kalvin counted five adult humans and four children, two boys and two girls. He moved to higher ground where he could see the lake and the thicket in the distance. Kalvin didn't see any more movement in the thicket. All the animals and probably most of the reptiles had left or been eaten by the creepers. Even the birds avoided the thicket.

The children had left the lake and were eating their lunch. All the men and one woman were still fishing. The other woman was eating with the young ones. Half an hour later all the adults had quit fishing and were in the camp. Kalvin watched as one of the boys walked into the woods in the direction of the thicket. The boy looked to be ten or eleven years old. Kalvin continued to watch the youth until a fox interrupted his thoughts.

"I just wanted to tell you that Kleatus and the other

monsters are okay," reported the fox. "There was quite a battle last night that involved six kudzu monsters and around seventy creepers."

"Were any monsters badly injured or killed?" Kalvin asked.

"The monster named Karl was bitten several times," answered the fox. "He was the one the creepers first attacked. Karen was the first monster to come to Karl's aid followed by Koda and Kokamo. Your Dad and Karrie arrived later. By then the creepers were retreating into the forest. Forty of them were dead. Five of the creepers tried to flee across a field, but Koda ran them down and killed them. He moves fast across flat fields."

Kalvin thanked him for the battle report and the fox trotted away. *Okay,* thought Kalvin, *That makes over eighty creepers dead so far. We're whittling them down. Wait a minute, where did that boy go? Did he go back to the camp? Kalvin had an uneasy feeling; he felt he should find the boy. Looking over the camp, he saw five adults, two girls and one boy. The other boy could be walking where the creepers are hidden.*

Kalvin moved through the forest in the direction of the thicket. He looked around for Squiggy and spotted him sleeping in a pine tree.

"Squiggy, I need your help!" Kalvin shouted. "A human boy wandered into the woods in the direction of the creepers. Run and jump through the trees and see if you can spot him. Alert the other squirrels you see."

I don't think the creepers will attack the young human, but I'm not certain. I don't see him anywhere in the thicket. He must be in the woods somewhere. Kalvin continued to travel through the forest at the slow pace of a kudzu monster. *He could be getting further away every minute,* Kalvin reasoned. *I'm three hundred yards from the camp. I don't think he'd wander this far.*

Kalvin kept moving through the forest until he was on the far end of the thicket. *I'm nearly half a mile from the camp. Where did that boy go? Where is Squiggy? Should I turn back or keep going?*

Kalvin stopped and scanned the thicket looking for the boy or creeper activity.

"Kalvin!" Squiggy barked. "You need to follow me and hurry as fast as you can move!"

"What's wrong?" asked Kalvin.

"The boy," panted Squiggy, "he climbed a tree and creepers have him surrounded!"

Kalvin hurried through the forest following Squiggy.

"Why did he climb a tree? He could've outrun the creepers."

"The creepers had him surrounded. He climbed the tree, closed his eyes, folded his hands and murmured words."

"He was praying." Kalvin remembered what Maranda had told Kandi about praying to God for help. "I hope we're not too late!"

Chapter Seven

A Boy in the Forest

Kalvin followed Squiggy until he spotted the boy about fifteen feet up a tree. The young human was sitting on a thick limb with his legs hanging down. He was facing two creepers that had climbed the tree. Three more were on the ground trying to grab his legs with their long vine-like tentacles. Saliva drooled from their mouths as they got ready to feed on the boy. The lad was fighting off the two creepers with a hunting knife. They tried to grab hold of the youth's arm but he was too fast for them. He slashed their tentacles with the knife blade. Their black blood dripped down the tree from their wounds.

I guess these creepers didn't know not to mess with humans. The creeper queen won't be happy with them.

Kalvin was twenty yards away from the boy. He drew back his upper left arm and threw the single-bladed axe at the creeper closest to the youth. The axe stuck in its back and the creeper dropped to the ground dead. Kalvin engaged the three creepers on the ground and sunk the blade of his other axe into the biggest one. The two remaining creepers grabbed his axe handle and Kalvin's arm. He began striking the two creepers with his lower arms. He tried to free the axe and his arm, but the creepers had their other legs wrapped around several bushes. Kalvin couldn't pull free of the creepers' grip and he couldn't reach the single-bladed axe in the dead creeper.

The youth continued to fight the creeper in the tree. He had succeeded in slicing up three of the creeper's eight tentacles, and one of its eyes dripped black blood. The creature broke off the attack and began climbing down the tree.

The other two creepers were taking a terrible beating, but were afraid to let go of the arm holding the axe. The injured creeper left a black smear down the tree trunk and attacked Kalvin from behind. Kalvin slapped at the injured creeper with his upper left arm tentacle as the creature crawled up his back. Out of the corner of his eye Kalvin saw the young human throw his knife. Kalvin felt the creeper jerking around as it dropped from his back. The creature landed on Kalvin's back feet tentacles.

One of the creepers let go of Kalvin's arm and fled toward the thicket. Kalvin jerked the other creeper into the air slamming it against the tree trunk. The creeper was stunned and turned loose of the axe handle. Kalvin's double-bladed axe sailed through the air and killed the creature that was fleeing toward the thicket. He turned and pulled the other axe from the first dead creeper. The stunned creeper tried to escape but Kalvin chopped it with the axe. The creeper that was on his back was squirming on the ground. Kalvin raised his axe but the creeper died before he could strike it.

Kalvin watched the young human climb down the tree. The boy's clothes were stained black with creeper blood. The youth pulled his knife out of the creeper and wiped off the blade on some grass.

Squiggy climbed up to Kalvin's shoulder. "There's a man headed this way and several other people in the forest."

"R.J., where are you!" the man shouted out.

The lad placed the knife back in its sheath and ran toward the sound of the man calling his name. Kalvin was going to warn the young human not to tell what happened, but the boy was gone. Kalvin's lower arms grabbed creeper legs and he began to drag the bodies into the forest. He could hear the man talking to the young human.

"Where have you been?" the man asked. "We've been searching the forest for you."

"I had to climb a tree to escape giant spiders!" R.J. exclaimed. "I prayed for help and God sent a tree creature to help me!"

"What are you talking about?" the man shouted. "Giant spiders… tree creature…and what's that black stuff on your shirt and pants?"

"I think its spider blood. I killed one with my knife and the tree creature killed four of the giant spiders with his axes."

"That's the story you're going to tell your mom? Chastity is going to skin you alive when she sees your clothes. You better come up with a better story."

Kalvin had dragged all the creeper bodies into the woods, covering them and the blood trail with leaves and dirt. R.J. took the man to the tree. The black blood was on the tree, but Kalvin and the dead creepers were gone. Kalvin watched them walk away while R.J. tried to convince the man that dead giant spiders were there a few minutes ago.

Sorry I had to do that to R.J., but I don't want the humans finding dead creepers, Kalvin thought. *If the adults found the creeper bodies, then they might believe R.J. about the walking tree that fought with axes. The fewer humans that know about us the better. I wonder if R.J. was right when he said God sent me to help him. Anyway, his prayer was answered.*

Kalvin returned to the spot where he could watch the humans at the lake and spotted his little sister hidden in the bushes.

I knew she couldn't resist spying on the humans. She just had to get a closer look.

"Squiggy, go tell Kandi that I said for her to quit spying on the humans and go back on top of the cliffs."

Kalvin watched Squiggy deliver his message. Kandi said something to Squiggy, and then continued to watch the camp.

A few minutes later Squiggy was back on Kalvin's shoulder.

"Kandi said that you're watching the humans. If you can watch them, she can too."

I love my sister, thought Kalvin, but she can drive me crazy at times.

The humans were still there at night. They cooked over fires and told stories. R.J. told about his encounter with the giant spiders and the tree creature that carried axes. Everyone enjoyed his tale, but no one believed him. The next morning the humans packed up and left the lake.

Kalvin returned to the thicket to see what the creepers were up to. The creepers continued to wait in the thicket.

Maybe they're not moving because of all the human activity over the last two days. But I think they're planning something.

All of a sudden Squiggy got excited. "I see my daughter jumping through the trees and coming toward us!"

"Sparkle probably has a message from Kandi," Kalvin replied. "It must be important. She's jumping from limb to limb like something is chasing her."

Sparkle scrambled to the ground and ran up to Kalvin.

"Kandi spotted a large number of creepers headed your way," panted Sparkle. "Kandi said they're scattered all over the forest, more than she's ever seen."

Chapter Eight

The Creeper Queen

Kalvin sent Sparkle back to Kandi and sent Squiggy with a message to inform his mother about the large number of creepers.

He moved further into the woods away from the thicket and climbed to the top of a hill near the cliffs where Kandi was watching. Kalvin could see the thicket which was about three hundred yards away. Past the thicket dozens of pairs of round yellow eyes shone in the forest. Also there were two pairs of larger round red eyes.

Several thoughts sprang into Kalvin's head. *Karrie mentioned large red eyes. She said that the queen's drones had red eyes. The drones are large creepers that mate with the queen to produce more creepers. The drones are always close to the queen. I sent Squiggy too quickly. If I had waited, I could have told Mom the queen was near.*

Kalvin made his way up the path toward the top of the

cliffs. *I need Kandi to send Sparkle to Mom,* he thought. *The queen must be in the forest and we can't let her get to the big lake.*

Kandi must have spotted Kalvin because she hurried down the path to him.

"Kandi, the queen's drones are in the forest. That means the queen is down there."

"I'll send Sparkle to alert Mom, Dad and the others," she said. "Maybe you should stay up on the cliff with me until they arrive."

"Good idea, Kandi. We'll be safer up there and we can still watch the thicket and the forest."

Kalvin and Kandi moved to the cliff top and watched as two drones emerged from the forest. They both were around nine feet long. They were taller than the other creepers and had a dozen long leg tentacles covered with red leaves and thorns.

Kandi made a gasping sound. "Look there in the forest!" Kandi pointed with her arm.

Kalvin saw it -- a large pair of red eyes. The eyes were about three feet above the ground. They were round in the center and tapered to a point on the ends. The queen slowly emerged from the forest. She stood about five feet high and was fifteen to sixteen feet long. She was black and covered with greenish-black moss. Her sixteen legs were tinted red and had long red thorns two to three inches long. The queen and the drones had yellow teeth but their teeth had a green furry growth on them that made them look moldy.

Those teeth look poisonous to me, thought Kalvin. *I'll have to ask Karrie about them.*

A mist was forming in the thicket giving it a spooky appearance. Scores of creepers began to leave the forest and enter the thicket. Their slow walk made them appear as if they were walking under water. The queen moved to the middle of the thicket and squatted down. The drones moved toward both ends of the thicket. Around a hundred creepers had emerged from the forest and surrounded the queen. Their legs arched up to form a dense barrier of legs around the queen. Dozens more of the creepers spread out in the woods that bordered the thicket on three sides.

"I wonder why the queen doesn't enter the lake?" asked Kandi. "She's only about four hundred yards from it."

"I don't know, Kandi. It could be she's afraid of being seen by the ranger station. Or maybe she only hides in the lake when she's in danger. But if she decides to move toward the lake, we'll need everyone to stop her."

A few minutes later Squiggy and Sparkle ran up the path to Kalvin and Kandi.

"The monsters are on their way," Squiggy reported. "Your mother should be arriving soon."

By noon Kleatus and Kitty were at the top of the cliffs with them. Kokamo arrived an hour later.

"When Karl and Karen get here, we need to move down the hill into the woods between the lake and the creepers," Kleatus stated. "I don't see any creeper activity in that part of the forest."

"Do you think the ranger can see us from his tower? After all, it's daylight," added Kalvin.

"Oh, Karrie forgot to tell you," said Kokamo, "the ranger has known about us for years. Karrie must have figured Karl or Karen had told you about the ranger."

"No one told us," said Kandi. "I've been trying to hide from him during the day."

"Karl and Karen should arrive in a couple of hours," said Kokamo. "Koda is waiting for Karrie to join him and they should be here by late afternoon."

"Kandi, when we go down the hill, I want you and Sparkle to stay up here as lookouts. If you see anything unusual send Sparkle to warn us," said Kleatus.

"Everything I've seen today looks unusual," answered Kandi.

"If you see creepers trying to sneak behind us or something like that, send Sparkle to let us know," said Kitty. "But don't come down from the cliffs. Stay up here no matter what happens to us. Promise me you will stay up here."

Kandi didn't say anything. Kitty continued to stare at her. Finally Kandi gave her word. "Okay I'll stay up here no matter what happens, I promise."

Late that afternoon all the monsters were in the wooded area between the lake and the creepers, except for Kandi.

Koda spoke to the monsters. "I'll take the center and the rest of you spread to either side of me about ten yards apart from each other. Karrie, you take the end of the right side and Kalvin, you take the end of the left side. That will put Kalvin closest to the cliffs and his sister. The queen will head for the lake once the fighting begins. We can't allow her to enter the lake."

"How about the queen and her drones; are their teeth poisonous?" Kalvin asked.

"Their bite is somewhat poisonous," answered Koda. "But it's not as dangerous to kudzu monsters as it is to the animals. When we attack, we'll go in a "V" formation. I'll take the point of the formation with Karl, Karen and Karrie on my right and Kleatus, Kitty, Kokamo and Kalvin on my left. If the creepers get behind us, close the "V" and form a circle."

While Koda was speaking, a creeper scout spotted them and sounded an alarm. Shrill squeals sounded from dozens of creepers. A minute later there was complete silence. Kalvin didn't hear a bird whistle or a cricket chirp. All Kalvin heard was the wind rustling the tree leaves. Then the queen rose up in the thicket and issued a loud shriek. Thirty creepers and the two drones moved to guard the queen. Another hundred and fifty creepers began to surge toward the lake and the kudzu monsters.

Chapter Nine

Creeper Horde Attack

Koda moved quickly in front of the other monsters and began to engage the creepers in combat.

"Squiggy," Kalvin yelled, "watch my back and keep an eye on Kandi. Let me know if she's in danger."

My arms are starting to tremble and my heart is beating fast, thought Kalvin. *It must be from fear of all those creepers. There are nearly twenty of them for each one of us. They'll swarm all over us.*

By the time the other monsters reached Koda, the creepers had covered him like ants. Koda crushed one after another with his massive arms and tossed their bodies to the ground. He bled from dozens of wounds but they didn't seem to faze him. Soon all the monsters were swinging axes and clubs at the creepers. The creatures couldn't get past their defense.

"Kalvin, look behind you at the lake!" Squiggy shrieked.

Kalvin turned and saw that dozens of creepers had emerged from the lake.

Oh, no, the queen must have known we were here. She was waiting for all the monsters to get between her and the lake so she could spring her trap. We're completely surrounded by creepers.

"Karrie, Kokamo, creepers are attacking from the rear!" Kalvin shouted.

Kalvin, Karrie and Kokamo turned toward the lake and closed the "V" formation. Kokamo took the middle with Karrie and Kalvin on either side. Kalvin moved the axes to his lower arms.

"Squiggy, look behind me again and tell me if the other monsters move forward," Kalvin said. "Climb on top of my head. It's the safest place to be with all these creepers."

Around fifty creepers had come out of the lake. The monsters weren't moving; they stayed in place and chopped at the creepers. The creepers' favorite targets were the feet tentacles of the monsters. Kalvin killed several creepers biting on his tentacles, but they still managed to bite him half a dozen times.

"Form a circle," shouted Koda. "Everyone move closer together and face outward. There are too many of them for us to move forward. I'm leaving the formation to make sure the queen doesn't enter the lake."

Koda circled around the other monsters as the fighting continued. Kalvin saw a sea of creepers surrounding them. Creepers climbed over other creepers to get at them. Yellow teeth were snapping everywhere he looked. Axes and clubs hammered the creepers as the monsters desperately tried to keep the creepers from breaking their circle.

Out of the corner of his eye, Kalvin saw various animals attacking any creeper that ventured into the forest.

There are so many of them, thought Kalvin. *How long can we hope to hold them? If they break through our circle, they'll attack us from behind.*

The queen, her two drones and her guard of creepers remained out of the battle. Around a hundred and seventy creepers were still attacking the eight kudzu monsters.

Koda left dead creepers everywhere he went. Creepers had quit attacking him and were trying to bring down the other monsters. All the monsters were bleeding, but none were seriously hurt.

Kalvin and the others had been fighting for thirty

minutes when the sun set. Around seventy creepers were dead or badly injured. The monsters had moved even closer together making it harder for the creepers to break through their circle.

The creepers began to coil their tentacles around the monsters' arms. Kleatus and Karl were just barely able to swing their weapons with creepers hanging onto their arm tentacles. Kokamo swung one of his axes, but the other had too many creepers for him to lift. Kalvin and the females couldn't lift their weapons at all and the creepers concentrated their attack on the monsters that couldn't lift their arms. Creepers were getting inside the circle and biting the back legs of the monsters.

When Koda killed one of the creepers hanging on Kalvin's lower left arm, Kalvin raised his left arm enough to bring his axe down on the other creeper. He then killed a creeper on his right arm and two other creepers jumped away from him.

"I'm moving inside the circle," Kalvin said. "I'll start killing the creepers biting us from behind."

As Kalvin moved inside the circle, everyone slid toward each other and closed the circle again. Kalvin chopped a creeper biting his mother's feet and another one on her right arm. He killed one attacking Karen's feet, then turned and saw two creepers chewing on one of Karrie's back feet. Kalvin chopped down with both axes and killed the creepers on Karrie. Sadly, she was too badly wounded. Her back feet couldn't support her and she toppled backwards. Kalvin caught her with his upper arms but the creepers swarmed over her. Kokamo had freed his other axe. He knocked creepers off Karrie with one axe and fought the creepers that attacked him with the other. Kalvin sliced creepers with his axes until there weren't any left on Karrie.

Kleatus killed several on Kitty and Karl was killing them on Karen. Over a hundred of the creepers were dead on the battlefield. Kleatus and Kitty stood back to back as they fought behind and to the right of Kalvin. Karl and Karen were back to back and to the left of Kokamo. Koda was crushing any creeper he could catch.

The queen and her creeper guard tried to head for the lake, but Koda kept moving in front of her. Most of the creepers began to lose heart. Their attacks grew fewer and weaker as they moved back from the group of kudzu monsters. The monsters spread out and began attacking the creepers.

Only fifty of the attacking creepers were alive after an hour of fighting and they fled toward the forest or joined the queen's guard. Thirty were still with the queen and they were joined by twenty more. The other creepers and the drones scattered into the forest. The queen and her escort exited the thicket and fled into the forest. Koda, Kokamo, Karl and Kleatus pursued them.

All right! We have them on the run, Kalvin rejoiced.

Squiggy had left with Kleatus so he could go through the treetops and keep watch on the queen. Kitty and Karen bound Karrie's wounds and held her upright.

"Kalvin, wait a minute; I don't want you to take off," Kitty told him. "Let me bandage some of the bites on your feet and arms."

"I'm okay, Mom. Your wounds look worse than mine."

"Karen and I will bandage each other's wounds later. Now hold up the feet that are bleeding."

While Kitty wrapped his feet, Kalvin spotted some wounded animals in the forest. Kitty finished doctoring Kalvin and started bandaging Karen.

Kalvin entered the woods and picked up several wounded animals. He carried them to his mother. Kitty bandaged their wounds while Karen finished bandaging Kitty's feet. Kalvin held Karrie up so she could rest and feed. Another thirty minutes passed.

When Karen finished treating Kitty's wounds, she took Kalvin's place. Leaning on Karen, Karrie hobbled about the battlefield. Kitty continued to apply salve to the wounded animals.

"I'm glad Maranda's mother gave us these good bandages, Kitty said. "They stay on us better and are easier to put on the animals. Karen, Karrie and I are staying here for awhile to care for the wounded animals. Kalvin, I want you to check on Kandi and make sure she's all right. Be careful; some of the creepers ran into the forest."

"Where is the raccoon that was assigned to you? You need to send him to me if you're in trouble," Kalvin replied.

"Rascal was in the forest fighting the creepers. I'm sure he'll be back soon or Charlie will return. Karen can send her squirrel. Scooter is still with her."

"If Rascal isn't back when Squiggy returns, just keep Squiggy with you. Do you want me to bring Kandi back with me?"

"Yes, I think you should do that."

Chapter Ten

The Battle Continues

Kalvin walked a quarter of a mile to the lake and looked up at the cliff. It was dark and he could barely make her out. Kandi seemed to be throwing rocks over the side of the cliff. Something large was climbing the cliff and two large creepers were at the foot of the hill going up to the cliff top.

Kalvin hurried toward Kandi. *Where is Sparkle? Kandi should have sent us a message that she was being attacked.* Suddenly four creepers emerged from the forest to the right of Kalvin. When the creepers attacked, he angled toward the lakeshore. Kalvin got a better look at the creeper on the face of the cliff. It was one of the drones.

The four creepers were between two and three feet long. Kalvin ran along the shore ahead of them but he was slowed down by his bandaged feet. The creepers were gaining on him. Normally, Kalvin would have gone to meet them, but he wanted to get to Kandi as fast as he could. The drone was about halfway up the hundred-foot cliff. Luckily, it couldn't climb fast and the two large creepers were waiting on the path and not attacking Kandi.

Kandi still has her hatchet and the four-foot pointed stick she called her spear. She could give the drone a good fight, but he's still twice her size. He switched his thoughts to the large creepers on the hill. *They must be waiting for the drone to attack. Then they'll surprise Kandi from behind.* Kalvin's thoughts were interrupted when a creeper grabbed one of his back feet. He stopped, aimed and threw his single-bladed axe into the creeper's head.

I couldn't stop and fight the creature; the other creepers would've caught up with me, Kalvin reasoned. *I'm nearly to the path that leads up to the cliff top, but I have to hurry to stay ahead of the creepers.*

Kalvin started up the path. The two large creepers were around five hundred feet away and still watched Kandi drop rocks on the drone. *Maybe the creepers don't like drones. They don't seem concerned that rocks are bouncing off its head and back.*

Once again Kalvin's thoughts were interrupted by a creeper hanging onto his foot. Kalvin turned enough to see the creeper and chopped off the leg that held him. But the other two had caught up with him. One of the creepers let out a shriek. *Oh, no, now the two large creepers will be headed this way.*

The three smaller creepers were not attacking. They sat and waited for the bigger creepers to join them. Kalvin spotted a small poplar tree near him. Although he hated to kill a tree, he chopped it down with one swing. Kalvin cut it at an angle so the bottom of the tree and the stump had a sharp point. The tree gave him another weapon. He backed a little ways off the trail so he could see all the creepers. The small creepers were on his left side and the two large ones on his right.

Kalvin glanced up the hill. He couldn't see the face of the cliff, but the tip of a creeper tentacle was at the top of the cliff. The five creepers were very close to him. Kalvin jabbed at the three creepers with the pointed tree trunk. The small creepers jumped back. Kalvin turned as the large creepers charged. He plunged the pointed tree trunk into one of the large creepers, pinning its body to the ground. Kalvin reached down with his lower right arm and grabbed a tentacle of the other large creeper. He jerked the creeper into the air, swung him over his head and slammed him onto the pointed stump of the tree.

A small creeper bit his foot just before Kalvin killed it with his axe. The other two creepers fled down the path. The two large creepers were thrashing about with large wooden stakes stuck through them.

Kalvin looked up the hill to Kandi several hundred feet away. She battled a drone that was twice her size. Several tentacles were wrapped around Kandi's middle as she chopped at them with her hatchet. Every time the drone tried to pull Kandi toward its teeth she jabbed him with her spear. Kalvin pushed up the hill as fast as he could travel. Very few trees were on the hill, so he made good speed despite the pain in his feet. Kalvin was about three or four hundred feet away when the drone wrapped a tentacle around Kandi's spear. Kandi struck the tentacle with her hatchet and the drone released her spear.

Kalvin knew that sooner or later the drone would take the spear away from her. Standing at the edge of the cliff, the drone couldn't retreat without falling off into the lake. The large creature whipped three legs at Kandi's spear just as she threw it. The spear stuck in the drone's left eye. It let out a loud scream of rage and surged forward.

Kalvin was less than a hundred feet away when the drone sank its teeth into Kandi's left front arm. She shrieked in pain from the bite.

Kalvin lifted his axe and hurled it toward the creeper drone. The axe sliced the side of the foul creature and the blade sank into the ground. The drone let out a shrill cry and pulled Kandi toward its gapping mouth. Before it could bury its teeth into Kandi, she struck its head with her hatchet. With a spear in its eye, a gash in its side and a hatchet stuck in its head, the drone backed over the edge of the cliff.

Kalvin's outstretched arms were only a few feet from Kandi when the drone fell from the cliff. With tentacles wrapped around her, Kandi was dragged over the side. Kalvin hurried and peered over the edge. He saw Kandi shoving the spear deeper into the drone's eye as they fell toward the dark water.

Chapter Eleven

The Search for Kandi

The drone and Kandi made a loud slapping noise when they hit the water. They sank below the surface for a few seconds; then Kandi floated up. She stayed there for a while before tentacles wrapped around her and pulled her under.

Kandi wasn't moving; she must be unconscious. I need to jump before the drone can bite her again. But I'm much heavier than Kandi. If I hit the lake bottom, it could kill me.

Those thoughts raced through Kalvin's mind as he set his feet to jump. Suddenly, Kandi popped to the surface again. There weren't any tentacles wrapped around her, but she still wasn't moving. She began to slowly float away from the cliffs.

Kalvin picked up his axe and started down the hill. He

looked around for Sparkle, but didn't see her anywhere. Kalvin hoped she didn't get eaten by a creeper.

When he reached the lake, he waded into the water and headed toward the spot where Kandi fell. Kalvin was only in water a little over four feet deep when his foot touched the body of the dead drone. *It's a good thing I didn't jump off the cliff; I would've hit the lake bottom.*

As Kalvin looked for Kandi, he saw something floating about a hundred feet from him. He fell over in the water and began rowing toward it with his four arms. Kalvin neared the object and saw it was just a floating log.

I don't see anything that looks like Kandi, but I can't see very well floating on my back. I need to get out of the lake and on my feet again.

Kalvin looked for a good spot on the lakeshore to get out. He spotted a weeping willow tree he could pull up on and rowed toward it. In a few minutes he had reached the tree and pulled himself to his feet on a low limb. He walked along the edge of the lake in the direction Kandi had been drifting.

The beavers and otters are in their burrows sleeping or have left the area, so I can't count on them for help. Where is she? I saw that creeper bite her on the arm. Kandi might be bleeding to death.

Kalvin scanned the lake and looked along the shore. He spotted something floating in a bed of cattails. He drew near. It was Kandi! She was still unconscious and green blood stained the water. Kalvin reached out with his lower arms and lifted her from the lake. He packed mud into the gash to slow the flow of blood. Kalvin pulled up long grass from the water and wrapped it around her wound.

The mud and bandage have stopped the bleeding for now, but I don't know how long it will hold. I need to get her to Mom as soon as possible.

Carrying Kandi, Kalvin hurried to where he had last seen the female monsters. He noticed a pair of yellow eyes in the forest on his right. Kalvin lifted Kandi to his upper arms and gripped the axe in his lower right arm tentacle.

The creeper is just watching me. I don't think he'll attack unless he has more creepers to help him, he reasoned.

Keeping a watch on the creeper, Kalvin continued toward his mother. He knew he must be getting close to the area where the humans had camped. His mom and the others would only be about a quarter of a mile past that. A second creeper joined the first as they angled closer to him.

At that moment a strong tentacle seized his lower left arm! Kalvin turned and saw the red eyes of the other drone. Its teeth were bared as it surged forward from the lake. Kalvin switched the axe to his upper left arm and Kandi to his upper right arm. He turned to face the drone and chopped down on the creeper tentacle. The axe blade severed the drone's tentacle and it fell to the ground. The other creepers were on his left side now. Kalvin pulled a bush out of the ground with his lower left arm. With his eyes on the drone, he blindly swung the bush back and forth. He felt the root ball hit one of the other creepers.

Kalvin backed and turned to where he could see the two small creepers and the drone. He roared a war shout and woke the squirrels. They began to chatter and bark. Kalvin pulled up another bush with his lower right arm.

Mom probably heard my shout and can locate me from all the squirrel chatter. Karen will stay with Karrie, but they will probably head this way. I just need to fend off these creepers until Mom arrives.

The creepers hissed at Kalvin and wrapped tentacles around his lower arm. The small ones were on his left, the drone was on his right and Kalvin's back feet were in the lake behind him. Kalvin used all his strength and swung his lower left arm. The creepers were jerked off the ground and crashed into the drone knocking the large creature sideways into the lake. As the creepers released his arm, Kalvin threw the bush. It hit the drone as it tried to crawl from the lake. Then Kalvin swung his axe and chopped off a creeper's head.

While the drone came out of the water to join the other creeper, Kalvin backed up on the path. He glanced at Kandi and saw she was slowly bleeding again. She had been dangling in one arm while he fought the creepers. Kalvin used both his upper arms to carry her and pulled up another bush.

Wounded and carrying his two-hundred pound sister, Kalvin felt weak and tired. He'd been fighting part of the day and half the night. Kalvin backed into a tree as the small creeper moved to get behind him. The drone advanced slowly and came to a sudden stop. An axe whirled past Kalvin, landing in the drone's eye.

Kalvin turned and threw his axe at the creeper in the woods, pinning it to a tree. The drone thrashed about and tried to pull the axe from its eye. Kitty stepped past Kalvin and struck the drone with a large club. The drone died from the blow, and Kitty turned to take Kandi from Kalvin's arms.

"The drone bit her, Mom. Not this drone, but another one. She killed it by herself and it dragged her off the cliff. I don't know what happened to Sparkle; she wasn't around."

"Sparkle and some other squirrels attacked a creeper in the woods behind Kandi. The squirrels were fighting the creeper when you were fighting the other creepers. She told me what happened then left to help Squiggy follow the queen," Kitty replied as she washed Kandi's wound. "I don't think the fall injured Kandi other than knocking her out cold. The real problem is the drone bite. I'll put some healing salve on her arm and a good bandage to stop the bleeding. I think she'll be better in the morning."

"Karrie should know something about treating a drone bite," said Kalvin.

"Karrie left with Karen to check on the male monsters. She was worried they might need urgent care."

Kitty bandaged Kandi and carried her back to where the wounded animals rested. Kalvin left to retrieve his other axe. When he got back to Kandi and his mother, Sparkle was there.

"Sparkle was telling me that the queen and some creepers are hiding in a small lake," said Kitty. "She also told me that Squiggy has been badly injured."

Chapter Twelve

Pursuit of the Queen

A few hours before dawn all the animals had been bandaged and departed for their homes. Kalvin, Kitty and Kandi followed Sparkle toward the location of the other monsters. Kalvin walked beside his mother as she carried her unconscious daughter in her arms.

"Do you think Kandi is any better?" Kalvin asked.

"It's hard to tell at this point. Hopefully Karrie knows something that will get rid of the poison in her arm."

I wonder how Squiggy is doing, thought Kalvin. *Sparkle didn't say what had caused his injury.*

They followed Sparkle for over a mile. Dead creepers were scattered along the way. They had only been dead a few hours, but their legs looked like shriveled vines and their bodies had gone flat.

The dead creepers look like shaggy door mats, thought Kalvin. *There can't be too many of them still alive, two or three dozen at best, plus the queen. Sparkle said she was hiding in a small lake. I wonder how long it will take the creepers to eat everything in the lake.*

When they arrived at the lake, Kalvin noticed that Karrie was propped up with two posts made from tree trunks. She was resting and feeding while the other monsters tried to chase the queen out of the lake. The lake was about two hundred feet wide and four hundred feet long. Kokamo was at one end and Koda was at the other end. Karen carried two large boulders as she came out of the forest. She stretched back her arms and hurled them into the lake one at a time. While she did that, Kokamo went into the forest for rocks and boulders. Koda was hurling stones as quickly as Kleatus and Karl could gather them. Kalvin noticed his dad and Karl carried more stones and bigger boulders than Karen and Kokamo. Koda hurled a five or six hundred pound stone to the middle of the lake as easily as a human would throw a baseball.

"Kalvin, you go help gather stones with Kokamo and Karen. I'm staying with Karrie, Kandi and Squiggy," Kitty stated.

Squiggy, I'd forgotten about him! Kalvin spotted Squiggy curled up on some grass between Karrie and Kandi. A bloody bandage covered one leg and his breathing was heavy. He was sleeping, so Kalvin didn't want to wake him. Smitty, the squirrel that was with Kalvin last year, was resting close to Squiggy.

"Smitty, are you okay?" asked Kalvin.

"No!" He barked. "A darn creeper bit off the tip of my beautiful tail!"

"I'm so sorry, Smitty," said Kalvin. He knew squirrels were very proud of their tails. They often showed emotion with their tails, like flipping them back and forth when they were angry. Sparkle used to be so shy she would cover her face with her tail.

Kalvin was angry at the creepers as he searched for large stones to bombard the lake. Hours passed as the monsters hurled hundreds of stones into the lake. The water level of the lake had risen several inches since he had been there. Kalvin learned from other animals that only six creepers entered the lake with the queen. A few fled into the forest and some of them were killed by the animals. They said the drones escaped too, but Kalvin already knew what happened to them.

Kalvin came out of the forest with his lower arms loaded with rocks, but the other monsters weren't throwing stones. He set his rocks down and scanned the lake. Two men were fishing at the far end of the lake. Kalvin stood still and sent his feeder roots into the ground.

Well, I can sure use the rest. I wonder if the fisher-men are going to catch any fish. The queen and the other creepers have been down there for twelve hours.

Kalvin noticed something mossy floating on the water. It was a dead creeper. The men didn't seem to notice it or they didn't know what to make of it. The fishermen only caught a couple of small fish by late evening, so they packed up their gear and left. Half an hour later the monsters were bombing the lake again.

Karrie woke up shortly after Kalvin and his mother had arrived that morning. She had Kitty gather some things to dress Kandi's wounded arm. Kandi was awake when Kalvin checked on her that night. Both Kandi and Karrie were doing better. Squiggy was still sleeping, but his breathing was steady. It was a good sign that he was getting better.

Kalvin had to go farther from the lake to find more rocks. But they continued to bomb the lake all night. In the morning they stopped throwing boulders and circled the lake about two hundred feet apart. They took turns sleeping. Every other monster would sleep for four hours then the others would sleep. The forest animals joined them and helped keep watch. For three days they kept watch on the lake. Kandi was better and stood next to Kitty. Kalvin had given her his single-bladed axe since her hatchet was lost in the large lake.

Squiggy was up and hobbling on his bad leg. Sparkle gathered nuts and berries for him to eat. Karrie's fox, Charlie, came limping in one night. He and several foxes had fought and killed a creeper.

The queen and what's left of her escort have probably eaten everything in the lake. They will have to come out in a few days and we'll be ready for her.

Around midnight of the fourth night, two creepers emerged from the lake and attacked Kitty and Kandi. Two others surfaced and attacked Kalvin. They moved to either side of him hissing and wrapping their tentacles around his lower arms.

Just then the water began to churn and the queen erupted from the lake in a spray of water. She rushed onto the shore straight at Kalvin!

Chapter Thirteen

A Queen-Sized Battle

The queen veered to Kalvin's right and the two creepers clung to Kalvin's lower arms. He quickly killed one of the creepers with a chop of his axe. Kalvin turned to fight the other creeper and the queen moved past him into the forest. The creeper opened its mouth to bite as Kalvin's axe sliced a deep gash across its back. Kalvin looked toward his mom and saw that the creepers that had attacked her and Kandi were dead.

Turning in the direction the queen had fled, Kalvin saw her disappearing into the dark forest. He pushed after her and heard another creeper hiss at him as he entered the woods. Kalvin threw his axe and killed it. By the time he retrieved his axe, the queen had disappeared.

Those creepers are sacrificing their lives so the queen can escape, Kalvin thought. *She'll head for the large lake. I need to find her, slow her down or stop her somehow. She shouldn't be able to move fast because of her large size. I may be able to catch her before she gets to the lake.*

Sparkle raced ahead of him to keep tabs on the queen.

"Sparkle, chase her through the trees; it's too dangerous on the ground!" Kalvin shouted.

He was sure Sparkle heard him, but she continued to run on the ground.

She's staying on the ground so she can travel faster, Kalvin thought. *I hope Sparkle's keeping an eye out for creepers hiding in the forest.*

A few minutes later Sparkle ran to him and climbed up on his shoulder.

"You need to go to your left more," Sparkle said. She jumped to the ground and ran after the fleeing queen.

The queen is trying to lose us in the forest. The woods will slow down the big monsters, but it's not going to slow me down.

 Several minutes later Sparkle returned.

"Don't go left anymore," she said. "Continue straight ahead; you're gaining on her."

In a few seconds Sparkle was gone again. A few minutes later Kalvin heard her yelling for help. He pushed as fast as he could go toward her shouts. She was in a small tree with a coyote jumping up at her. Kalvin roared and the coyote took off at a run.

Well, that warned the queen that I'm near, but it also let the monsters behind me know where I am.

Sparkle ran up to his shoulder.

"The queen is a few hundred feet in front of you," she chattered. "Can you see her?"

Kalvin could make out her black shape as she twisted through the forest.

"Sparkle, help guide the closest monster behind me. I'll need help when I catch the queen."

"I'm staying with you," Sparkle replied. "You can continue roaring to guide the other monsters."

Females! Kalvin thought, *They always argue with me. Why do they always want to argue?*

Kalvin gave a loud battle cry and continued to chase the queen. The queen made a shrill screech.

I bet she's calling any creepers nearby to come to her aid. The lake is less than a half mile away. If more than one creeper attacks me, I'll never be able to catch her.

The queen made a slight turn to her right and moved

into the thicket where the battle was fought. Kalvin roared and the queen shrieked as they raced over dead creepers.

The queen's moving faster, but so am I, Kalvin thought. *I'll catch her in a few minutes, but then what? I could chop off part of her leg, but she has sixteen. Chopping off a leg won't stop her.*

The queen was nearing the end of the thicket. The lake was only two hundred yards away and Kalvin was still fifty feet behind her. Kalvin pulled back his upper right arm and threw his axe. It flipped through the air and stuck in the queen's back. She screamed in pain and her massive body turned to face him.

An unarmed Kalvin slid to a stop twenty feet from the queen. Kalvin heard Kokamo's war shout as he entered the thicket a few hundred yards behind him. The queen paused for a second then turned and headed for the lake. Kalvin gave chase once again. He pushed and pulled forward as fast as he could go. The queen was less than a hundred feet from the lake and Kalvin could almost touch her. He thrust forward with his back feet and fell forward. As he hit the ground he grabbed two of her feet with his upper arms.

The queen began to drag him over the ground. Kalvin held onto a small tree with his lower right arm and grabbed a shrub with his lower left arm tentacle. The queen struggled to move forward. The shrub pulled out of the ground and the tree began to break.

The queen realized she wasn't going to make it to the lake before Kokamo caught up to her. She twisted, but couldn't reach Kalvin with her teeth. Whipping two of her thorny back tentacles around Kalvin's upper right arm, she pulled hard. The tree cracked. Kalvin felt himself being dragged toward her gaping mouth as she angrily ground her yellow and green teeth together. Kalvin still held the shrub and threw it at her face. The bush hit her but didn't stop her pulling. Kalvin reached out with his lower left arm and grabbed a large bush.

The queen wrapped another tentacle around his arm and tugged harder. The bush began to pull loose from its roots, and long red thorns scratched bloody grooves in Kalvin's arm. Kokamo roared again. He was a couple of hundred feet away.

A second war shout roared from the thicket that Kalvin recognized as his dad's. The queen became desperate. She rose up, flipped onto her back and landed on top of Kalvin. The axe was still in her back and the other side of it dug into Kalvin's back. She still couldn't bite Kalvin, so she turned onto her side. Letting go of the bush and her left leg, Kalvin was able to roll out from under her. They were lying back-to-back and facing opposite directions.

Kalvin still held one leg that now was stretched across the queen's face. The queen shrieked in anger and bit off the leg Kalvin was holding. She rolled away from Kalvin onto her stomach.

Okay, I need to crawl away from the queen's teeth, Kalvin reasoned. *If I can climb onto her back I can retrieve my axe.*

Kalvin rolled onto his stomach and quickly moved toward her rear. The queen pushed to her feet and faced Kokamo while Kalvin climbed onto her back. Kokamo only had one axe and a club left. He swung the axe and buried the blade into her side. She screamed, lunged forward and sank her teeth in Kokamo's arm.

Kalvin pulled forward and grabbed his axe. As he slid off the queen's back onto his feet, he pulled his axe free. Kokamo slammed his club on the queen's back and she released his arm.

Kalvin could see his dad fighting three creepers that had answered the queen's shout for help. Karen emerged from the forest to his right and hurled stones at the queen. Kalvin was the only monster between the queen and the lake. The water was a few feet behind him. Karl entered the forest and killed the last creeper attacking Kleatus.

The queen tugged at Kokamo's axe in her side pulling it free of her body. She swung the axe at Kokamo and clipped some kudzu off his chest. Kalvin swung his axe and sliced a large gash across her back. Turning toward him, the queen swung her axe at him. As Kalvin blocked her blow with his axe, the head of Kokamo's axe broke off. The queen struck Kalvin's arm with the homemade axe handle and knocked his axe into the air.

The queen threw the handle striking Kalvin on his chest. For a moment Kalvin was stunned as she hurried past him toward the water. He fell forward and grabbed one of her legs again, slowing her as she dragged him across the sandy shore. Kleatus hurled his mauls at her. One chopped off a leg and the hammer end of the other bounced off her back. The queen began to pull into the water.

"Kalvin, turn the queen loose," shouted Kleatus, "and get out of the way!"

Kalvin let go and rolled away, crawling toward a tree. As he pulled up he could only see the top of the queen's back as she disappeared into the lake. Just then a rusty steel train rail went sailing over his head and slammed into the queen's back. Black blood spewed into the air as she sank beneath the water.

Chapter Fourteen

Creeper Revenge

Kalvin watched the dark lake water turn darker. He didn't know who threw that steel rail until he turned around and saw Koda standing a hundred yards away. The queen must be dead, he thought. Wait a minute; where is Sparkle? Kalvin had forgotten about her in the heat of battle.

Kalvin's mother and Kandi came out of the forest. Sparkle was on Kandi's shoulder.

Koda came lumbering toward Kalvin.

"Where did you get that steel rail?" asked Kalvin.

"There's an old train track near here that hasn't been used in thirty years," Koda rumbled. "Most of the steel had been carried off, but I found that one in the bushes. Good job on slowing the queen down. If you hadn't delayed her, she would have escaped into the lake again."

"Thanks," said Kalvin. He was bursting with pride over Koda's praise.

Koda waded around in the water, but couldn't find the queen's body. In the morning Koda sent an otter into the lake to look for the queen. A few minutes later the otter came out of the lake and ran to where the monsters were gathered in the forest.

"I saw the queen," reported the otter. "She's about a hundred feet from shore and she's not moving. There's a big piece of metal stuck in her back."

"How deep is the water?" asked Koda.

"Oh, it's very deep in the middle of the lake," answered the otter.

Koda put an arm tentacle over his eyes. "How deep is the water over the queen?" he asked.

"The water is about half your height," said the otter.

"Keep a sharp eye out for humans," Koda told the others. "I'm going to wade out to the queen."

Koda followed the otter toward the queen. When he was about seventy feet from shore, he started moving very slowly. A minute later he shouted he'd found the queen and she was dead. All the monsters gave a sigh of relief. With the queen dead, that was the end of the creeper migration north.

"The queen is dead!" Karrie announced. "I think everyone should return to my hill and rest for a few days or weeks."

Over the next few days everyone talked about his or her part in the battle. Most of the adults had seen more fighting than Kalvin, but he had battled the biggest and fiercest of the monsters. Everyone was impressed with Kandi taking on a drone and killing it, although it almost killed her.

Koda stayed at Karrie's hill for nearly a week then left with Kokamo. Kokamo's arm was still bandaged and he'd always have a scar where the queen had ripped his arm open. Kandi had a scar on her arm from the drone bite that would be there for life. Half of one foot tentacle was missing on Karrie. She would have a limp for the rest of her life. Squiggy had a permanent limp, too, because of his mangled leg. His days of running messages were over.

Karl and Karen left a few days after Koda and Kokamo. Kalvin and his family stayed another week before telling Karrie goodbye. They promised to visit her every spring. Kleatus and Kitty decided to visit with Karl and Karen for a few days, but Kalvin and Kandi set out for home. Squiggy rode on Kalvin's shoulder and Sparkle on Kandi's. It was nearing the end of June as Kalvin and Kandi traveled a familiar route toward home.

"I'm glad that's over with," said Kalvin. "We'll never have to face creepers again. What creepers are left will be making their way back to the swamps."

"I'm glad we don't have to fight them again," answered Kandi. "I hate creepers. They're just plain evil. Let's walk all day and night; I want to get home as soon as possible."

"I know how you feel, Kandi. But we're eight or nine days from home and we need our rest."

They rested and fed all day and started out again that night. Kalvin had decided to keep the two axes until they reached home. He had an uneasy feeling after all that fighting and kept glancing around as they walked.

"Why do you keep looking behind us and in the forest?" Kandi asked.

"I'm not sure," he answered, "I feel like we're being followed."

"You are being followed," replied a raccoon hidden in the forest.

"What's following us?" Kalvin asked.

"I don't know," the raccoon answered. "They're ugly looking creatures with sharp teeth."

"Creepers followed us!" exclaimed Kandi. "Not all of them headed back to Florida."

"How close are the creepers to us?" Kalvin asked.

"They're very close," answered the raccoon.

"Kandi, there's a large oak tree ahead. I'm giving you the single-bladed axe and putting you on that large limb. You'll be ten feet off the ground. Hold onto the branch above you with your back arms."

"Creepers can climb the tree," answered Kandi.

"I know, but they'll have to get past me first. If they do make it up the tree, only one at a time can attack you on the limb."

"That's true," answered Kandi. "But one could climb above me and attack me from above."

"Maybe they won't think of that," Kalvin replied.

Kalvin put Kandi in the tree and the squirrels climbed to the treetop. Squiggy barked that he could see creepers.

Kalvin spotted a pair of yellow eyes in the forest. Then a second and third pair appeared. The creepers waited and watched. Kalvin knew they were waiting for other creepers. Soon there were six creepers and still they waited. A few minutes later four red eyes appeared in the dark forest.

Oh, no, two drones are out there! Six creepers and two drones, we're doomed!

Chapter Fifteen

The Last Battle

Squiggy and Sparkle started barking. The bark was echoed through the woods by other squirrels. The two drones emerged from the forest. They were smaller than the other drones. One was about eight feet long and the other was around seven feet. The six creepers moved through the woods on either side of Kalvin. Two of them moved behind him. Kalvin clutched the axe tight in his upper right arm tentacle.

All the creepers started to close the circle around Kalvin when, all of a sudden, animals erupted from the forest! Four foxes attacked one of the creepers and half a dozen raccoons attacked another creeper. Dozens of squirrels jumped on the two creepers on Kalvin's left side. Two possums and a weasel joined the fight. Even rabbits were attacking the creepers.

The two drones eased closer to Kalvin. They didn't

seem as confident of victory as they were a few seconds ago. Kalvin heard the two creepers behind him climbing the tree. He swung his axe behind him and felt it hit one. He heard the creeper fall to the ground and black blood stained his blade.

The seven-foot drone charged him. Kalvin swung his axe down and split its head open. The other drone hissed and wrapped two tentacles around his axe handle. Yanking on the handle, the drone pulled Kalvin away from the tree. Kalvin reached out with his left arms and clung to a small tree. He could see Kandi fighting a creeper above him. Kalvin began rocking the small tree back and forth as he tried to uproot it.

The drone wrapped two more tentacles around the handle and pulled closer to Kalvin. The drone's teeth were inches from the arm that held the axe. Kalvin pulled up a bush with his lower right arm and swung it at the drone. The root ball of the shrub hit the drone in the mouth and knocked it backwards. Kalvin uprooted the tree and swung the root ball at the drone's head. The drone jumped back before it hit him.

A dead creeper fell out of the tree and landed beside Kalvin. Then Kalvin saw the other axe whirl past him and the blade struck the drone on its back. The drone shrieked in pain and Kalvin pulled his axe free from its grip. He chopped down and hit the drone's head, killing it.

The foxes and raccoons had killed the creepers they had attacked and were chasing the last two through the woods. The two fleeing creepers were bleeding from dozens of small animal bites.

Neither Kalvin nor Kandi had gotten bitten during the fight. None of the squirrels or other small animals were badly injured. The foxes and raccoons returned to report that the other two creepers were dead. Though they had taken some bites, none were serious. Before the animals departed, Kalvin and Kandi thanked them for saving their lives.

"Okay, now I think we've seen the last of the creepers," said Kalvin. "I guess they knew I was the one that kept the queen from the lake until the other monsters arrived. They wanted to revenge the death of their queen."

"Let's just get as far as we can from here," answered Kandi. "I want to go home!"

Kalvin, Kandi and the squirrels ambled toward their home and put the creepers behind them. They reached home in a couple of days and rested a day before going to see Maranda and her parents.

Kalvin listened to Squiggy and Sparkle in the trees chattering about the battles to the other squirrels. Squiggy exaggerated his role in the battle a little more each time he told it. Maranda and her parents were happy that their gifts had helped the monsters in the battle.

A week later Kleatus and Kitty arrived home and learned about the last battle. They were thankful all the small forest animals had helped Kalvin and Kandi.

The rest of the year was very peaceful. As a matter of fact, the next five years were peaceful in the forest. Squiggy still rode on Kalvin's shoulder and Sparkle rode on Kandi's. Kleatus stopped growing at twenty-three feet. Karl and Karen had a daughter named Klara.

Early one spring Kalvin paced back and forth mumbling to himself.

"Why are you pacing about and muttering to yourself?" asked Kandi.

"I'm eighteen today," answered Kalvin. "I feel it's time I left home and explored new territory."

"Okay, you're rehearsing what to say to Mom and Dad."

"Well, every male monster leaves home around my age."

Kalvin stopped talking as his parents came into view.

"Happy birthday!" shouted Kleatus.

"Thanks, Dad," he answered.

"Thanks, Mom," he said. "I'm eighteen today, nearly sixteen feet tall and I weigh over a thousand pounds. I feel I can handle any danger in the forest on my own."

"Oh, Kalvin," cried Kitty. "You're leaving home, aren't you?"

"Mom, I want to explore other places. I want to experience new things."

"Where are you planning to explore?" asked Kleatus.

"I thought I'd go up to the Carolinas and maybe Tennessee," Kalvin answered.

"How long will you be gone?" asked Kitty.

"I was thinking a year or two," Kalvin replied. "I know you'll miss me and I'll miss you, but it's something I have to do."

"I know," his parents answered together.

"I've been dreading this day all year," whispered Kitty.

"I'm not leaving until tonight. I want to say goodbye to Squiggy."

"He's an old squirrel and has been sick," said Kleatus. "He may not be around when you return."

Kalvin saw that Kandi looked like she wanted to cry, but she didn't have any tear ducts.

"Don't be sad, Kandi,' he said. "Maranda will be home from college this summer and you can visit with her. You have your squirrel friend Sparkle. Maybe Mom and Dad will take you to see Karl and Karen's daughter."

"Did you forget her name again?" answered Kandi. "It's Klara."

"I remembered her name," he stammered. "You can explore the woods together. She's nearly your age."

"I'll be eight in six weeks," Kandi answered. "Klara just turned four. In fifteen years maybe we'll be close to the same age."

"You know you like being with her," Kalvin replied.

"She's okay for a day or two. But she gets on my nerves asking endless questions."

"Now you know how I felt when you were a small monster," Kalvin grinned.

Kalvin gave her a hug and pushed into the forest to see Squiggy.

I'm going to miss everyone, Kalvin thought. *But this is something I've wanted to do since I was eight years old. Adventures await me and, who knows, maybe I'll find a female that I like who likes me.*

THE END

LaVergne, TN USA
27 December 2010

210174LV00006B/8/P